Jeff Noon is the author of *Needle in the Groove*, *Vurt* and three other novels. His short stories have featured in several anthologies, and he is the author of the short fiction collection, *Pixel Juice*. He recently relocated from Manchester to Brighton.

Illustrator **Daniel Allington** used to live in England. He likes green tea, Vladimir Mayakovsky, and Katsushika Hokusai. He doesn't like white coffee, Francis Ford Coppola, or Bertolt Brecht. In his spare time, he teaches English as a Foreign Language.

D1568491

Also by Jeff Noon

Vurt
Pollen
Automated Alice
Nymphomation
Pixel Juice
Needle in the Groove

Cobralingus

Metamorphiction by Jeff Noon

Illustrated by Daniel Allington

Introduction by Michael Bracewell

CODEX

Cobralingus

by Jeff Noon

Published in 2001 by
Codex Books, PO Box 148, Hove, BN3 3DQ, UK
www.codexbooks.co.uk

ISBN 1 899598 16 2

Graphic design by Peter Pavement
Cover by Daniel Allington and Peter Pavement

Printed in Hong Kong

THE METAMORPHICTION OF JEFF NOON
by Michael Bracewell

Deep in the heart of Jeff Noon's fiction there seems to lie the ability to translate psychology and emotions into a landscape charted by the flexing or mutating of language. In what is arguably one of his most important short pieces, 'Crawl Town', Noon comes close to redefining the literary territory explored by Edgar Allan Poe and, later, Borges, through the refracted, tragi-comic story of fate and curiosity in a terminally post-industrial settlement. Like Poe's 'House of Usher', the town of Crawl becomes a psychological allegory, disturbingly fixated on notions of imprisonment and escape.

But 'Crawl' finds Noon at his more naturalistic. As a prose stylist, Noon deals in terms of voice and tone, locating the feelings within his characters and then pitting them – more often than not – against a set of circumstances or a pre-determined condition which will shape their particular destiny. In this sense, Noon is a classicist, usually working within the understood conventions of Greek or Shakespearean drama. He then relates this classicism to a radical index of style and language.

More than any other writer of his generation, Jeff Noon has assimilated the techniques developed in the recording of music and pioneered their literary equivalents. As a writer for whom literary style is paramount, he is therefore concerned with the creation of a synthesis which will test the usual functions of language and text. In many ways, Cobralingus can be read as a report on this process, which doubles – via its own self-programming, so to speak – as a kind of metaphysical confession, channelling a powerfully felt vision.

The conceptual thinking behind Cobralingus (as explained in Noon's 'Instructions') could be seen as a conflation of self-regenerative recording systems (a comparison would be Brian Eno's Discreet Music (1975)), the apparatus of literary deconstruction (here the comparison could be with The Lover's Discourse of Roland Barthes, or the literary 'crossings' of Harold Bloom) and the signage of computer gaming or information technology. What emerges form this conflation of concepts, however, is a wholly organic use of literary process.

Noon is not concerned with technique for the sake of technique; he is not a 'systems' artist in the accepted sense. Rather, as explored throughout his prose, he is concerned with the relationship between language, psychology, image and narrative, as those qualities can be animated by reactive internal devices. Much of Noon's best known imagery – from *Vurt* and *Pollen* through to the more naturalistic styling of the stories in *Pixel Juice* – derives its power from the literalising of poetic language and the concretising of images: the sudden opening up, within the landscape of the prose itself, of new routes to character and narrative, enabled by altering the meanings of words within the containers of their language.

With this visceral extrapolation of literary 'style', Noon creates a method of writing in which language itself becomes subject matter and action. Hence, in the earlier development of his fiction, the application of 're-mixing' and 'dub' which have led to the multi-tasking devices of *Cobralingus*.

In the past, Noon has spoken of the inspiration which he has found for these processes from the push towards the musical abstraction of electronica within dance music. The music of Pole, or Autechre, therefore, can offer some insights into Noon's approach to his literary systems. The term 'systems', however, suggests a coldness; *Cobralingus*, on the other hand, is a set of systems and devices which trigger the warmth and imaginative fancy of classic romanticism. Noon is recognised as a writer who can pursue existing, given phenomena and articulate their future; he has even coined the term 'post-future', to denote a period when the whole idea of the future has ended.

This notion of pursuing a phenomenon to its untested next stage, and allowing it to declare its own rules and logic, is central to the present volume. The texts emerging from the systems of *Cobralingus* can be described as sexually reproductive texts; fused and synthesised, each development of Noon's 'word-snake' creates a text which is pregnant with its successor. The fecundity of this system permits the writing to discover, in turn, its own internal systems – creating sonnets from an 'inlet text', or transposing a list into a graphical device. In terms of critical theory, Noon is extending such literary experiments as Derrida's *Glas,* but releasing the ensuing text, as poetry, from the clinical conditions of pure experiment.

Ultimately, *Cobralingus* is Noon's response to the deep romanticism of many of its 'inlet' texts, from Herrick and Shakespeare to Emily Dickinson. And perhaps, in creating the system of a 'word-snake' to almost depersonalise the processes of writing, Noon has created the literary apparatus which most enables him to find himself.

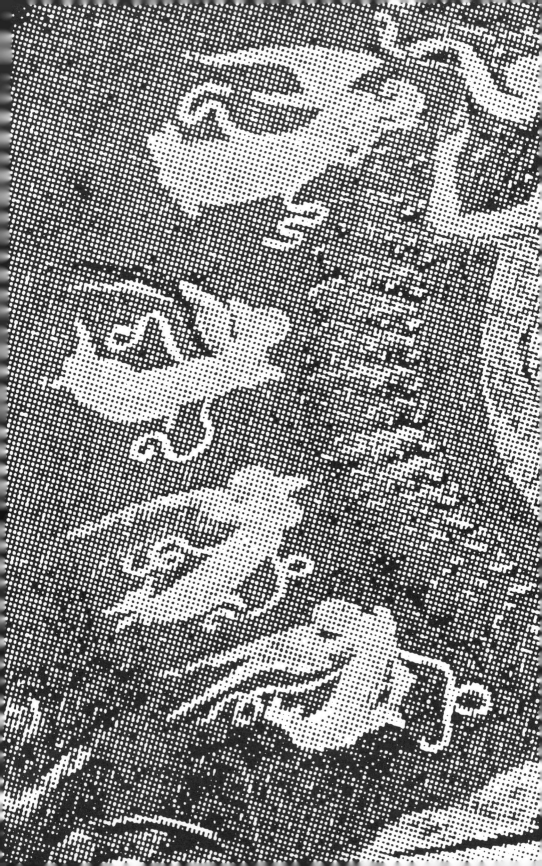

COBRALINGUS

CONTENTS

COBRALINGUS

The Cobralingus Engine allows the user to manipulate language into new shapes and new meanings. The device takes an **INLET** text as a starting point, which is then processed to create another text entirely, known as the **OUTLET**. This outlet text can be seen as the ghost, or the unconscious desire, haunting the original text.

The Cobralingus Engine makes use of the Metamorphiction process. This process imagines text to be a signal, which can be passed through various **FILTER GATES**, each of which has a specific effect upon the language. Each gate allows the writer to access different creative responses within his or her imagination. The effect of each gate is to produce an **INTERIM** text, which is transmitted further along the pathway. For instance, Mary Shelley's *Frankenstein* contains the following sentence: 'I saw the dull yellow eye of the creature open.' This text could be pushed through the **RANDOMISE** gate, producing: 'I lulled open the creature of the eye's low way.' We could then **ENHANCE** this, by changing *way* into *direction,* and by adding another letter 's': 'I lulled open the creature of the eye's slow direction.' The words can be altered in these and other ways until, finally, the outlet text is created. This progress is entirely dependant on the user's inspiration, moment to moment, as the text makes its journey through the machine.

This book contains various examples of the Cobralingus Engine in operation. In each case a **WORD-SNAKE** diagram allows the reader to follow the transformation of the text as it travels from gate to gate. Along the way it is hoped that each interim text will be of individual interest; however, the real pleasure of Cobralingus comes from enjoying the pieces as a whole. From inlet to outlet, the journey is the goal.

INSTRUCTIONS COMPLETE

We hope you enjoy using the Cobralingus filtering device.

COBRALINGUS: KEY TO FILTER GATES

START
> Denotes that the Cobralingus device has been activated.

INLET
> The start-up text. The initial signal on which the device will act.

CONTROL
> Brings the text down to earth. Forces language to behave itself.

DECAY
> Gently breaks down the text. Dissipates. Introduces corruption to the signal.

DRUG
> Injects artificial stimulant into the language. Type of drug will always be specified.

ENHANCE
> Creates elements of beauty.

EXPLODE
> Breaks up signal into highly disordered fragments. To be used with caution.

FIND STORY
> Forces text into the nearest possible narrative, however nonsensical.

GHOST EDIT
> Kills the text. Calls up a ghost to haunt the language.

HOLD
> Temporarily halts the Cobralingus process.

INCREASE SENSE
> Significantly enhances text. Increases readability.

MIX

Combines all elements into a single entity.

OVERLOAD

Drastically increases image density of text. To be used with caution.

PLAY GAME

Mischief maker. Encourages craziness. Results may surprise the user.

PURIFY

Loses deadwood. Selects images or phrases from the text.

RANDOMISE

Disorders text. Parts of text may be lost or changed.

RELEASE VIRUS

Attacks text, changing words of choice into others of a similar sound. Recommended for advanced users.

SAMPLE

Introduces new element to signal. Source of sample to be specified.

SEARCH & REPLACE

Uses machine function to introduce new elements to text. Elements always specified. For example, 'Search and Replace: *day* with *night.*'

OUTLET

The final result of the filtering process.

SAVE

Denotes that the Cobralingus device has been deactivated.

MOTH: They have been at a great feast of languages, and stolen the scraps.

COSTARD: O! they have lived long on the alms-basket of words. I marvel thy master hath not eaten thee for a word; for thou art not so long by the head as *honorificabilitudinitatibus.*

William Shakespeare, *Love's Labour's Lost*

'Plucke the fruite and tast the pleasure'

Rosalynde's Madrigal

Plucke the fruite and tast the pleasure

    Youthful Lordings of delight,

Whil'st occasion giues you seasure,

    Feede your fancies and your sight:

        After death when you are gone,

        Joy and pleasure is there none.

Thomas Lodge, 1591

                                    e as
                         h
                  e   a t
            e   e   u a a   h   a
       uc ke th efruu ea nta thp le as u
       l luckeethhefruuitteantaastthpleeasu e
       p lpluckeetheffruiteeandttasttthepleasurere   r
       p pyyyouthhulloorddigsoffdelighhhtuutre r
  y   yyouthfulllorrdingsooffdeliiighttghtthtu u
  w   w yhilsstococassigiuuesyoseuuree e   r
       w hilstooccasiogiuessyouuseasureee p e   u
  h h ffeedeeyoufaanciiesndyurrsiighhtte   l   s a   e
       f eedeyyourrfanciesaandyyourssightt t
       e e eaafteerdeeathhhenyuaaregonee e
  a   afterddeathhwhennyouaaregone
       a   ajjoyy **apple** easuuristheernnoone   n
       o oyaanddpleasureisthereejno o n
       o   aa nd leea s l sth e re no
            a   e   s s h   e
                 e   h
       e

wake up; Julie; bed; Badger Cat; Radio One; Kevin Greening Show; Spice
Cat; feed cats; breakfast; fruit and fibre cereal; milk; tea; coffee; cats out;
read newspaper; The Observer; news sections; aftermath of report into the
Stephen Lawrence case; sports section; Henman and Rusedski win
Guardian Direct doubles final; Manchester United 2 Southampton 1;
Chesterfield 1 Manchester City 1; review section; Gilbert and George article;
Sarah Kane suicide; new Underworld CD; book reviews; Shakespeare: the
Invention of the Human, Harold Bloom; Into the Looking Glass Wood,

```
                              e as
                 h
              e    at
           ehfruite  ue ea a nha
          uckeethhefruutean antathleas u
        l luckeethhefruitteantaastthpleeasu e
       p lpluckeetheffruiteandttasthepleasurere r
        ppyyyouthhulloorddigsofdelighhtuutreer
   y  yyouthfulllorrdingsoffdeliiighttghtthtu u
   w w yhilstococassigiuesyoseuuree e            r
    w hilstooccasiogiuesyouseasuree      p          e       u
  h  hffeedeeyoufanciiesndyurrsigh hte         l   s         e
    f eedeyyourrfanciesaandyyoursightt                  a
    e eeaafteerdeeathhwhennuaaregonee
      afterddeathhwwhennyouaaegone
      a ajjoy apple easuristhernoon n
       o oyadpleasureisthereejno on
       o  aand leea sl sthero
```

Alberto Manguel; work; Cobralingus; Tony arrives, lunch; ham sandwiches;
chocolate biscuits; photographs of Venice; work; Cobralingus; idea of
including everything I do today; listen to records; Pole, CD1; Porter Ricks,
Biokinetics; Time Team, Channel 4; Radio One Chart Countdown; 10
Written in the Stars; 9 Lullaby; 8 Fly Away; 7 Erase/Rewind; 6 Runaway; 5
Strong Enough; 4 Just Looking; 3 It's Not Right but It's Okay; 2 Tender; 1
Baby One More Time; out; car stereo; The Smiths, The Queen Is Dead; The
New Emperor Chinese Restaurant; Pork with Peking Sauce, Chicken in
Black Bean Sauce; jasmine tea; home; car stereo; country and western
tape; tea; check email; you have no new messages; bed; read; Box Nine,
Jack O'Connell; sleep

```
                                        wak
                                       e;
                                       jul
                           ie;bed;cat;ra di o;cat;fo
                           od;drink;tastethepleasure;new
                           s;football;tennis;manchester;revie
                           ws;arts;shakespeare;invention;huma
                           n;thelookingglass;tastethepleasure;
                           work;cobralingus;tony;talk;food;dri            p
                           nk;chocolate;tastethepleasure;p                        l
                           hotographs;venice;work;cobrali    e        a
                           ngus;ideas;everythingidotoday;                      s
                           music;biokinetics;tastethepleas      u            r
                           ure;tv;archaeology;radio;topten;              e
                           tenderisthenight;blur;car;thesmiths;
                           chinesefood fruit tastethepleasure;ho
                           me;countryandwesternsongs;talk;ch
                           eckingformessages;bed;warmth;r
                           eading;novels;kiss;love;jnoon
                           ;sunday;28/02/99;
                                   sleep
```

'the bird of paradise'

Blackley, Crumpsall, Harpurhey

The clouds of a late November storm have been blown to white remnants, high in a pale blue sky. Winter is here; the day is held in freezing stillness. Sunday lays sorrow on the heart; all the cobbled back alleys are empty. Tall grey bins have been left upturned at crazy angles, and some stacked timber, swollen with damp, is catching the pink light of the afternoon sun. A mongrel dog, its coat the colour of cigarette ash and its wet, square-bearded muzzle lowered to sniff the length of a wall, is trotting towards the main road – where shattered glass glints around the sides of a telephone box, and the low sweep of vivid turf makes a child's drawing of the new estate. This is north Manchester, cut from Collyhurst to Crumpsall by a tapering valley in miniature, which is obscured by scrub and brown saplings.

The male exhalation of a bus's brakes gives way to the rising drone of its engine, then a pause for the gears to change and the hiss of heavy wheels advances into silence. It is as though the people have locked themselves away from their neighbours; as though these mean houses are hiding their poor like a lie. Quiet streets of descending terraces, falling away to the floor of the shallow valley, where a formation of dust-coloured tower blocks has been set down on the cleared land. The sky looks vast above them. But ruddy Victoriana remains: the church of Mount Carmel, its mullioned west window like the stern of a dry-docked galleon; the old steam laundry, buttressed with engineering brick; three pubs; the damp husk of the Conservative Club. At dusk, the near future appears to intrude on this northern Gothic, in the calm, violet forecourt light of the big new petrol station on the Rochdale Road.

Lank and dark-eyed children play in thin clothes on the cold streets. Some bouquets of rusted flowers, their paper wrappings sodden, are wired to the low railings beside the pedestrian crossing.

Michael Bracewell, 1999

Clouds
white remnants held in a stillness
where Sunday lays sorrow on the heart,
swollen with a damp pink light.
A mongrel dog.
Cigarette ash
descending.

A child's drawing of Manchester,
cut from shattered glass.
A rising drone and hiss of heavy silence.
The estate has locked itself away.
Thin cold streets, hiding their colour
behind blown dust.

Male exhalation,
a dry galleon of steam,
engineering a church of sky.
The crazy angled husk of the Gothic Club.
Dusk, the near future.
Northern Violet.

Lank and petrol-eyed children play
in bouquets of rust formation.
Sodden flowers,
wired to the cross.

Dusk, the near future. Saturday night at the Rust Club, where Mongrel Gothic perform songs from their latest release, Bouquets of Drone. Female singer with the band, Violet Sky, hisses like a dog, remnants of notes held in a dry stillness.

Shakespeare Walk   Brontë Avenue   Wilde Street   Wordsworth Road

In the audience, white cigarette smoke caught in pink damp light, and a rising sound of husky male breath. Their hearts, locked tightly inside, engineering hidden colours in formations of dust, shaping their pain. A northern day's pain, the estate of love. Cut from heavy silence, descending, a glass shatters. Sunday morning lays sorrow on the heart.

Keats Crescent   Austen Walk   Coleridge Avenue   Ruskin Road

Outside the club, lank children play, dreams of petrol in their eyes. While, in the nearby churchyard, a lonely kid makes a drawing of Manchester, all crazy angels and swollen clouds. Sodden flowers, wired to a cross. His sister's grave.

Tennyson Gardens Waverley Crescent Milton Grove Chaucer Avenue

In the boy's mind, a dark galleon drifts by, steam-driven through these thin cold streets, into the sky. He sets fire to the drawing; flakes of carbon, mailed to the stars. Sunday morning lays sorrow on the heart.

Dusk, the near future, Satur n. G a the r here rel ic songs from the s ea. Bouquets of drone l inger with the violet k isses. A dog man s of t in a stillness,

shakes a re al   b on e venue   wild tree   word swor d.

In the d ence t igar smoke, ink a rising sound of sky. Le t the Eart h 's engine ring our n ation of dust, shaping the r ain. Or d ain the state of love, cut from heav en, descending. A glass sun d orning lays sorrow on the

k at scent   st alk   r aven   skin road.

The b lank child of petrol in the s hi n y church makes a wing man, a crazy angel cloud flow, wired to a rave

son ar   wave crescent   ton g   h aven.

In the boy's mind, a dark gall dr eam rive r gh o st. To the sky he sets the wing. Lakes of ar o ma. Le t the stars' g lays row the heart.

the compass

the lyre   the balance

the sails   the twins   the serpent

the dove   the net   the bird of paradise

the clock   the virgin

the telescope

At dusk, on the lakes of aroma, the people of Saturn gather relic songs from the mist. Along the parched shoreline, all the wild drone flowers linger with their violet kisses of scent. A dogman soft in a stillness, shakes a gentle word-sword in the circle of bone, conjuring out of dense tiger-smoke a rising sound of prayer. Together now, the people offer their songs to the engine of balance that shapes the virginal sky. Ordain the state of love, they sing, that heaven may descend in rain upon this, our paradise of dust.

At dawn, the dry glass sun lays sorrow on the planet. In the church of petrol a silent child watches a cat stalk a raven bird along the road of skin. In the boy's skull, a serpent girl sails a river of dreams, the ghost of his twin. The raven's dark shine of ink escapes into a tree of clocks. Seeing this, the boy constructs a wingman, cut from the strings of a lyre, a handful of drone petals, a net of wire, the plumage of a dove. Using telescope and compass, he sets a course through the ring of clouds, toward the distant Earth. Flow, my crazy angel, whispers the child, along the crescent of my tongue, along the sonar waves to your haven in the sky. Allow the glaze of stars to welcome your heart.

gather songs
        soft in a stillness of
    parched skin –
                in raven tongue sky
        violet drone   let rain descend
a circle of bone   heaven dust
                is conjuring ghosts –
        allow dark sky words
            ordain the state of love
        in sun sorrow –
                the silent child
of skull twin shine
            uses ink wing   and compass lyre
        to set a course
                in cloud flow –
                along the crescent
            of the tongue
        allow stars
            your heart

Along the crescent of the tongue allow
These words; allow the skull's incessant drone;
Allow that thought be conjured in the flow;
Allow that heaven twin the rounded bone.
Within the violet parched-out mouth a rain
Allow to fall, that voices dark and hoarse,
In fluid tones the state of love ordain;
Allow the heart's encompass set a course.
To silent lips give song as from the lyre,
In raven's ink the shine of stars outrun;
Allow the ghost, the skin, the sky inspire;
And soft in sorrow's cloud, allow the sun.
Allow that wings be fixed to every brow;
And every child of dust, a tongue endow.

SAVE

'redraft chemistry of the rune spell'

```
START
  |
INLET
```

Confessions of an English Opium Eater

As the creative state of the eye increased, a sympathy seemed to arise between the waking and the dreaming states of the brain in one point – that whatsoever I happened to call up and to trace by a voluntary act upon the darkness was very apt to transfer itself to my dreams; so that I feared to exercise this faculty; for, as Midas turned all things to gold, that yet baffled his hopes and defrauded his human desires, so whatsoever things capable of being visually represented I did but think of in the darkness, immediately shaped themselves into phantoms of the eye; and, by a process apparently no less inevitable, when thus once traced in faint and visionary colours, like writings in sympathetic ink, they were drawn out by the fierce chemistry of my dreams, into insufferable splendour that fretted the heart.

Thomas De Quincey, 1821

creative state
the eye increased
the waking
and the dreaming
states of the brain
call up the darkness
transfer my dreams
I feared Midas
turned to gold
defrauded
human desires
visually represented
shaped into phantoms
traced in faint
visionary colours
sympathetic ink
chemistry of my dreams
insufferable splendour
a fretted heart
Thomas De Quincey

a reactive test
    they serenade ice
weak night
    germinated hand
betroth fantasies
    the landscapes lurk
sad ferments marry
    if idea dreams
dug rotten old
    Freud dead
headism runes
    unseal led perversity
dominant phosphates
    infect radiant
silicon ovary ours
    synthetic kamp
deform as my chemistry
    if sabre found rune spell
eat the redraft
    o my sad technique

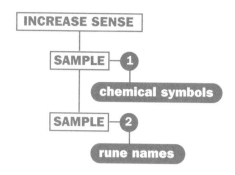

INCREASE SENSE

SAMPLE — 1

chemical symbols

SAMPLE — 2

rune names

Xe

sol

Cast the runes: London, 1936:   Eu

Sigmund Freud died tonight,   jara

singing a weak serenade of ice: Mo   ur

he betrothed fantasies: technique: nagal

digging up the landscapes of dream,   Cd   Se

where sadness lurks and ferments: Nd   gifu

ideas of the alchemical wedding: Zn

eat all those old and rotten dreams: pertra

science will unseal perversity: Cu

redraft chemistry of the rune spell: madr   tyr

now we let dominant phosphates   Mg

infect the radiant silicon ovary: lagu

test for reaction: germination   Au

of a deformed synthetic hand.   naud

Fe   odal

Ti   eoh

He

data

unusual

h   reload

computer   f

sex

CHEMICAL WEDDING:

GERMINATION OF A DEFORMED SYNTHETIC DREAM HAND

anagram

gay   rhizome

conjure

g

fluid

regulate   d

dna

I beheld the wretch –
the miserable monster
whom I had created.

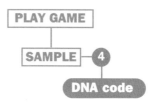

You are cordially invited to a

CHEMICAL WEDDING

* * *

Behold!

TAGTCGAAGC	**Mr Wretched Data**	*ACTTGTAACG*
ATACGTAGAC	**will take the monstrous hand of**	*TAGACCGTAC*
CATCGATTGA	**Miss Deformed Synthetic**	*GACTAGGCAT*
TCCGATGGTA	**in marriage**	*GTACCGTATG*
GTAGTCGATG	* * *	*AGTCGTAGTC*
CAGAGTCGTA	**Regulation Computer Sex**	*ACGTTGAGCA*
TATTGCACGG	**to be publicly germinated**	*GTAGTCGATT*
CGAGTCCAGA	**creating**	*AGCTGAGAAC*
ACCGTGATAC	**Unusual Dream Rhizomes**	*CTTAGTAGAA*
CATAAGTACG	* * *	*TAGTACCATG*
TCCAGATCAA	**Plus!**	*AAGTCCTAGA*
ATGGTACCAG	**Dancing to the sounds of**	*GTCAGACTGA*
CTTAGATCGA	**Dan Anagram DNA**	*TATGCCAAGT*
TAGGCGATCA	**& his Conjure Fluid**	*ACCGTAGACT*
CGAATAGTAC	**featuring Gay Miserable!**	*GATCGATAGA*

* * *

Réloadez S'il Vous Plaît

ACTTGTAACGATACGTAGACTAGACCGTACCATCGATTGAACTAGGCA
reloadanagram**DNAH**oldmonstrouschemicalweddingwretchedmi
serabledatasyntheticmarriageregulation**HAND**deformedcompute
rsexgerminatedcreatingunusualdreamrhizomesdancingconjureflu
idgayreloadanagram**DNAH**oldmonstrouschemicalweddingwretch
edmiserabledatasyntheticmarriageregulation**HAND**deformedcom
putersexgerminatedcreatingunusualdreamrhizomesdancingconju
refluidgayreloadanagram**DNAH**oldmonstrouschemicalweddingwr
etchedmiserabledatasyntheticmarriageregulation**HAND**deformed
computersexgerminatedcreatingunusualdreamrhizomesconjurefl
uidgayreloadanagram**DNAH**oldmonstrouschemicalweddingwretc
hedmiserabledatasyntheticmarriageregulation**HAND**deformedco
mputersexgerminatedcreatingunusualdreamrhizomesconjureflui
dgayreloadanagram**DNAH**oldmonstrouschemicalweddingwretch
edmiserabledatasyntheticmarriageregulation**HAND**deformedcom
putersexgerminatedcreatingunusualdreamrhizomesconjurefluidg
ayreloadanagram**DNAH**oldmonstrouschemicalweddingwretched
datasyntheticmarriageregulation**HAND**deformedcomputersexger
minatedcreatingunusualdreamrhizomesdancingconjurefluidgayre
loadanagram**DNAH**oldmonstrouschemicalweddingwretcheddata
syntheticmarriageregulation**HAND**deformedcomputersexgermina
tedcreatingunusualdreamrhizomesdancingconjurefluidgayreload
anagram**DNAH**oldmonstrouschemicalweddingwretcheddatasynt
heticmarriageregulation**HAND**deformedcomputersexgerminated
creatingunusualdreamrhizomesdancingconjurefluidgayreloadana
gram**DNAH**oldmonstrouschemicalweddingwretchedmiserabledat
asyntheticmarriageregulation**HAND**deformedcomputersexgermin
atedcreatingunusualdreamrhizomesdancingconjurefluidgayreloa
danagram**DNAH**oldmonstrouschemicalweddingwretchedmiserab
ledatasyntheticmarriageregulation**HAND**deformedcomreload
ATTGCACGGGTAGTCGATTCGAGTCCAGAAGCTGAGAACACCGTGAT

DRUG — metaphorazine

OUTLET

A

an

dnhana   dnaha

dnahan   ndhand

T   dhn   dnahan   ndnaha   G

dnahan   handna   adnaha

A   andnah   C   dnahnd   hnadna

dnahna   andnah   dnahna

handna   handna   T   andnaha

dnandh   nahandn   handnah

han   nahand   andnaha   andnaha

andn   dnahna   ahandna   dnahand

dnaha   handnan   dnahand   nandnaha   A

C   handn   handna   handnah   anahandn   andhan

andhan   andnahanhandnahanahandad   G   nahandn

andnaha   nanhandnahnadnahandnahan   C   dnanhan

dnahnad   nahandnahandndnaandnahad   nahandnh

dna   andnaha   handnadnahanandnahannadna   hanandhh   A

hanaha   ndnahanahandnadnahandnnadnadnahand   nhandnah

aandha   aandhandnadnaandnahandnahadnahandn   hnadnaha

nahandn   nhandnhandnaandnahandnahandnaandnahandandnahan

dnaand   dnahandnaandnahandnahandnahandnanahandnahand

nahandn   andnahandndnahandnahandnahandnahandnahandnah

andnahandandnahandndnahandnahahandnahandnahandnaha

ahnandnahandna handnahnandnahanhandnahannahandn

andhandnahandnahandnahandnahandnahanadnahn

dnaahandnahandnahandnahandnahandnahandn   T

ndnahandnahandandnahandnhandnahand

nahandnahandnahandnahandnahandna

nahandnahanddnahandnahnandnah

andnahandnahandnahandnahnah

andnahandnanahandnahandnah

andnahandnahandnahandnaha

ndnahandnahandandnahand

ACTGAATCGGTAGCGATAG

GCTTAGTCCAGAAGCTGA

SAVE

44

EXPLODING HORSE GENERATOR UNIT

'sets *fire* to the language and the whole *fucking* horse'

The Taming of the Shrew

Petruchio is coming, in a new hat and an old jerkin; a pair of old breeches thrice turned; a pair of boots that have been candle-cases, one buckled, another laced; an old rusty sword taken out of the town armoury, with a broken hilt, and chapeless; with two broken points: his horse hipped with an old mothy saddle and stirrups of no kindred; besides, possessed with the glanders and like to mose in the chine; troubled with the lampass, infected with the fashions, full of windgalls, sped with spavins, rayed with the yellows, past cure of the fives, stark spoiled with the staggers, begnawn with the bots, swayed in the back, and shoulder-shotten; near legged before, and with a half-checked bit, and a head-stall of sheep's leather, which, restrained to keep him from stumbling, hath been burst and now repaired with knots; one girth six times pierced, and a woman's crupper of velore, which hath two letters for her name fairly set down in studs, and here and there pierced with pack-thread.

William Shakespeare, 1592

RANDOMISE
|
ENHANCE

Petruchio is swayed, stark staggers, infected with the fashions in a new pierced sheep's-head hat. Shaking a spear. And a stumbling old pair of thrice taken-out, half-checked breeches. And a pair of shoulder-boots that have been candle-glanders. One buckled with a hilt, another laced in the town's stud-pack armoury. His jerkin hipped with an old gall's mothy saddle and stirrups, with kindred knots. Begnawn besides, with the speed broken. Troubled with the old spavin's thread-cases, and rayed with the old rusty yellows. Past coming cure of the six times five, so spoiled with the shotten-bots. With the one girth turned in the back, and before, with a bit of restrained repair. No stall to keep him from liking to mose in the near chapeless woman of velore. In the legged chine of leather, which hath two letters for her name fairly set down in lampass. Full of possessed horse, which, here and there pierced with wind crupper sword, with two broken points, hath been burst.

burst of new staggers

    candle points swayed   possessed

           saddle fashions pierced with legged head

arse lamp   spacing ray checked

   stark hat breeches broken shoulder

       stumbling old pair of boots that have half woman

           hilt pack jerking speed

cases full of here and there

     hipped an old gal's yellow chime

        old rusty troubled stirrups buckled

kindred gnawed velour knots

    cure two letters for her shaking name

       infected sword that laced the town's stud

 broken thread stalls repair

 coming cropper six times five   spoiled horse

     spear-shot turned bits and bots in the back

old moth glands

   pierced sheep's armour

         like to nose leather near chapels

set winds down in unrestrained girth

DECAY

SAMPLE — 1

racehorse names

burst of new stags pant way
       tumbling pair   half woman
posse sad fashion   leg rust stirs up buck
     to let us now shaking name   velonauts

              butterscotch
hip old gal's yell chime   *moon glow*
              never can tell   ass-head amp
             northern svengali   kid read gnaw cure
space-ray leather check   *prince consort*
              serpentine   infects word-hat ace-stud
star breech's brook   *square dancer*
com crop sex times fave   *nova city*
            vision of night   pie sheep amour
            first mistress   hot spear turn bit in the back
            poets pride

                 broke read no repair
     oil horse mother glands
      hit pack jerk speed
       wins down in unrest girl

RANDOMISE

INCREASE SENSE

Poets unrest! In burst of new fashion, halfway dancer tells stage-woman of sad times; prince is a jerk. Mother Leg stirs up gland-amp buck. Hot pants hit concert-speed, to let us name velocity rust. Hip old Scotch svengali's yellow moon-ray can chime, as head northern-ace girl kid reads cure for amour. Nova vision of spacenaut's leather-posse studies hatcheck pair. Red Star mistress reaches brook. Pet sheep-pack crop favourite sex pie, and first night spear turns back pride. Broke down, shaking, never in butter. Neither repair nor oil wins glow, as tumbling word serpent infects square horse.

SAMPLE 2 horseracing terms

photo finish   brood mare   each-way bet
under starter's orders   bloodstock
dead heat   flat racing   bookmakers
past the post   handicap   purebred

velocity poet orders unrest
burst of new fashion
halfway handicap name-dancer
woman of sad times
concert-stage prince is a jerk-bred bet
stirs up speed-gland sex amplifier
let us brood cure for dead amour
yellow butter moon-mist photo can chime past rust
nova-vision reaches north
pure heat-racing ace girl reads under blood red star
æther-posse studies nought-space
pie-ray squared no repair
hatchet-heads spear back pride
broken down word-oil infects shaking horse
serpent makes nightmare book
wins tumbling glow finish

Oh yeah, we went down the Circle Club last night, you know, the πr^2 joint? Should've seen it, they had this poet on stage, going speed-crazy she was, like a million words a minute. Like it's the latest thing, you know? Mind you, she was one sad-eyed dancer, this woman – one good leg, one bad – and she was like interpreting the words as they burst out. Now, the owner of the club, he's a right jerk-officer, you betcha life he is, straight down the line. He only tries to get the poet off stage, doesn't he, to bring on the stripper guy, get the old snake-glands powered up, you know? Only, the dancing poet, she don't wanna leave the stage, damn right. Crying out that she wants to find the cure for dead love, and making like a yellow butter moon-mist photo, or some such, like a chiming dance, way past corruption. Meanwhile the stripper's doing his utmost to play the sexy dumb-thing, but the nova-vision reaches the heights when the poet wheels on this horse. Yeah, man, a fucking horse! Like an artificial horse, made out of tyres and wires and plastic bags and stuff. And the poet, she's like a pure heat-racing girl as she reads out under the blood red lights. Now the audience, it's a bunch of air-heads mostly, yer basic zero-space posse, and they're going wild at the stage battle. The bouncers have to move in, hatchet-faced bastards one and all, and the πr^2, it's nearly destroyed beyond all repair, especially when the poet blows up the plastic horse. Oh yeah, I'm telling you, spews all this crazy mixed-up word-oil at the horse, sets fire to the language and the whole fucking horse just blows up right there on stage, splattering the poor stripper guy, the owner, and most of the audience as well. I tell you, man, it was like Shakespeare exploded. Like a word-serpent, making a nightmare book, and the poet wins a tumbling. Total glow finish. Horseshit, the place was maniac city.

we   the Circle
    poet   crazy   like a million words a minute
             sad eye danc
      ing   word   burst   er
of   straight   line   s
        trip   the   snake land power
know   the   Crying
     cure   dead love   making like a yell
or   like a ch   ance   orruption
   play the sex dumb   the nova vision
wheels   mad
   e   lastic   poet
reads out   the blood   of air   mostly
  zero
   hatchet   the r(adius)   destroy   all

          language
   blow up   splatter
      like Shakespeare exploded   word
serpent   night book tumbling   glow   Horseshit
   maniac

we the circling poem
straight line crazy like a million
words-a-minute sad

eye-dancing word burster
trip the snakeland power
know the crying cure

dead love making like a yell
or like a chance eruption
play the sex and dumb the nova

vision wheels
mad elastic poet
reads out the blood of air

mostly zero
hatchet the radius
destroy all language

blow up splatter like snaking spear
exploded word-serpent night book
tumbling glow horseshit maniac

Riders of the Purple Sage

Only a hundred yards now stretched between Black Star and Wrangle. The giant sorrel thundered on – and on – and on. In every yard he gained a foot. He was whistling through his nostrils, wringing wet, flying lather, and as hot as fire. Savage as ever, strong as ever, fast as ever, but each tremendous stride jarred Venters out of the saddle! Wrangle's power and spirit and momentum had begun to run him off his legs. Wrangle's great race was nearly won – and run. Venters seemed to see the expanse before him as a vast, sheeted, purple plain sliding under him. Black Star moved in it as a blur. The rider, Jerry Card, appeared a mere dot bobbing dimly. Wrangle thundered on – on – on! Venters felt the increase in quivering, straining shock after every leap. Flecks of foam flew into Venter's eyes, burning him, making him see all the sage as red.

Zane Grey, 1912

Only a hundred yards now stretched between Black Star and Wrangle, circling the poem, straight line crazy like a million. The giant sorrel thundered on – and on – and on. This words-a-minute sad eye-dancing word burster, with every yard he gained a foot. He was whistling through his nostrils, wringing wet, flying lather, and as hot as fire, and tripping the snakeland power, knowing the crying cure. Savage as ever, strong as ever, fast as ever, but each tremendous stride jarred Venters out of the saddle! His dead love making like a yell, or like a chance eruption of Wrangle's power and spirit and momentum, that had begun to run him off his legs. Playing the sex and dumbing the nova, Wrangle's great race was nearly won and run, on vision wheels. Venters seemed to see the expanse before him as a vast, sheeted, purple plain sliding under him, where the mad elastic poet reads out the blood of air. Black Star moved in it as a blur. Mostly zero. The grey zone, where the rider, Joker Card, appeared a mere dot bobbing dimly. Hatcheting the radius, destroying all language, Wrangle thundered on – on – on! Blowing up, splattering like snaking spear, Venters felt the increase in quivering, straining shock after every leap of the exploding word-serpent's night book. Flecks of foam flew into Venter's eyes, burning him, making him see all the sage as red, like a tumbling glow of horseshit maniac.

infected with the fashions
stark spoiled with the staggers
hath been burst and now repaired with knots
here and there pierced with thread

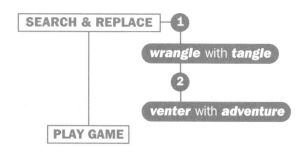

And it's only one hundred sentences to go now, with *Book of Night, Book of Night,* stretched halfway between *Black Star* and *Tangle,* and making a final crying cure, it's *Dead Love,* bringing up the rear. And circling around them all, here comes *Snakehorse Poem,* it's *Snakehorse Poem,* crazy like a burst of splatter. See now, the million flecks of word foam, dancing, thrown into the writer's eyes. Yes, it's the giant radius of *Snakehorse,* here and there pierced with thunder, overtaking *Word Adventure* now. But still going strong on the outside, it's *Spear Shaker,* all aquiver with shocks of sadness, strained at by the wringing, the whistling, the wet words, flying down now, along this burning, elastic course. Keep an eye on *Tangle's* power, as hot as fire, and tripping out on momentum spirit. But savage as ever, strong as ever, fast as ever, it's *Snakehorse Poem,* with every tremendous stride jarring words off the pages of his skin. And with every word lost, he gains two more, and loses another five. His riding like a thread of chance, running off the script. Stark spoiled with the staggers and dumb to speak in straighter lines, now gone nova, now supernova. Adventures in the hatching. Surely, this tremendous horse sees the expanse before him as a vast, sheeted, purple sheen of text sliding under. *Black Star* only moves in it as a blur, blown to mostly zero. Down to the grey zone, where *Joker Poet* rides alone, a mere mad dot of a word, spoken dimly. Destroy! he whispers, Destroy all known languages, infect with the tangle fashions! Until, after every leap of the word-hurdles, coming through at last, it's *Snakehorse Poem,* overtaking *Spear Shaker.* This great, great race, nearly won and run, on vision wheels. Exploding now through *Word Adventure's* eyes, making him see all the pages as read, finally, like a tumbling glow of pure, manic horseplay, it's *Snakehorse Poem, Snakehorse Poem!* Excreting madness all around him! Most beautiful horse, surely thou hath been ruptured, and now repaired with bloody language and knots of tangled hair.

In one hundred sentences, this book of night

stretched halfway between black star and tangle

finds a crying cure for dying love.

Encircling snake poem, crazy like a burst of splatter

with one million flecks of word foam

thrown dancing into the writer's eyes.

The giant radius here and there pierced

with spears, with shakers, with shocks of sadness

with elastic words, wet with power,

and stark spoiled with the sex, staggers,

and chances upon these few pages of skin.

And dumb to speak in straighter lines

adventures in the thread of text slide beneath,

moving as a blur, blown to mostly zero,

destroying, and then hatching language.

Language, infected with tangle fashion,

exploding, sees all these pages as read, finally,

like a tumbling glow of pure, manic horseplay,

producing madness all around,

ruptured, and now repaired

with bloody language

and knots of twisted hair.

From tangled threads this book of night entwines
    All stars so black that broken letters make;
And I am dumb to speak in straighter lines.
    A horse attacked by liquid flex of snake,
That tightens, softly round the words at first
    To gently force all shaking spears to break:
Then tighter still, until the script is cursed
    And here and there now pierced, elasticised,
Stark spoiled, staggering, finally – burst!
    And blown to mostly nought in readers' eyes;
Until with chance upon this splattered page
    A cure for dying love of words, now cries:
Infect the text! Inspect, reflect, enrage!
    Have sex! Let language fashion, fuse and breed,
Explode, and hatch anew; the horse engage
    With snake, that circles round itself to feed
The tumble flow. A manic prayer, ensnare.
    In wounds that plough the skin, the words proceed
To staunch themselves with seeds of cheap repair;
    The wreckage of the text itself together binds
From dregs and flecks, from knots of twisted hair,
    The tangled threads this book of night entwines.

SAVE

'the grubs are bursting the combs, grown obscene and serpentine'

Areas of the Moon

Mare Imbrium
Mare Fecunditatis
Mare Tranquillitatis
Mare Crisium
Mare Humorum
Mare Nectaris
Mare Frigoris
Mare Cognitum
Mare Nubium
Mare Ingenii
Mare Anguis
Mare Vaporum
Sinus Aestuum
Sinus Roris
Sinus Amoris
Sinus Iridum
Palus Putredinis
Palus Somnii
Palus Epidemiarum
Palus Nebularum
Lacus Mortis
Lacus Somniorum

Areas of the Moon

Sea of Rains
Sea of Fertility
Sea of Tranquillity
Sea of Crises
Sea of Moisture
Sea of Nectar
Sea of Cold
Sea of Knowledge
Sea of Clouds
Sea of Ingenuity
Sea of Serpents
Sea of Vapours
Bay of Heats
Bay of Dews
Bay of Love
Bay of Rainbows
Marsh of Decay
Marsh of Sleep
Marsh of Epidemics
Marsh of Mists
Lake of Death
Lake of Dreams

The Shipping Forecast

Viking: south or southeast 5 or 6 increasing 7, occasionally gale 8 in West. Wintry showers then rain, becoming moderate. **North Utsire South Utsire:** south-easterly 5 to 7. Wintry showers then rain. Good becoming moderate. **Forties Cromarty:** southerly 5 to 7, perhaps gale 8 later. Occasional rain. Moderate or good. **Forth Tyne:** southerly 4 or 5 increasing 6 for a time. Occasional rain later. Good. **Dogger:** south 5 or 6. Showers. Good. **Fisher German Bight Humber:** south-easterly 4 increasing 5 or 6, occasionally 7 in Fisher later. Mainly fair. Good. **Thames Dover:** south-easterly 4 or 5 decreasing 3. Mainly fair. Moderate or good. **Wight Portland Plymouth:** easterly 4 or 5 becoming variable 3. Occasional rain. Good becoming moderate. **Biscay:** variable becoming south-easterly 3 or 4. Rain at times. Moderate. **South Finisterre:** south-easterly 6 to gale 8 becoming cyclonic 5 or 6. Thundery showers. Good. **North Finisterre:** southeast backing east 5 or 6 decreasing 3 or 4. Rain then showers. Moderate or good. **Sole:** variable 3 or 4. Occasional rain. Moderate. **Lundy Fastnet Irish Sea:** south-easterly veering south-westerly 4 or 5, becoming variable 3 in South Lundy and Fastnet. Occasional rain. Good becoming moderate. **Shannon:** variable 4 becoming south-westerly 5 or 6. Showers. Moderate or good. **Rockall Malin:** south-westerly 5 to 7, but 4 at first in South. Showers. Good. **Hebrides:** southwest, backing south for a time, 6 to 7, occasionally gale 8. Rain then showers. Moderate or good. **Bailey:** southwest, backing south at times, 5 or 6, but variable 3 or 4 in North. Wintry showers. Good. **Fair Isle:** south 6 to gale 8. Showers. Moderate or good. **Faeroes:** southerly 5 or 6, occasionally gale 8 at first in East. Showers. Good. **Southeast Iceland:** southeast or cyclonic 4 or 5 backing northeast 5 to 7 in North. Wintry showers. Moderate becoming good.

```
MIX
 |
PURIFY
 |
ENHANCE
```

Ingenuity:
Moon of dreams 4 or 5 increasing 6, occasional love death 7. Moderate.

Nectar:
Mists 5 to 7, perhaps moisture 8 later. Occasional vapour lakes. Good.

North Fertility South Fertility:
Heats 5 to 7. Serpents, rising. Moderate becoming good.

Love:
Rainbows 4 or 5 increasing 6 for a time. Nectar later. Good becoming moderate.

Tranquillity:
A sea of mist 4 or 5 decreasing 3. Mainly cloud sleep. Moderate or good.

Serpent:
Heats 6 to vapour 8 becoming cyclonic 5 or 6. Nectar decay. Good.

Knowledge:
Cold moon 4 increasing 5 or 6, occasionally 7 in rainbow later. Good.

Crisis:
Cyclonic 4 or 5 backing vapour 5 to 7 in bay of heats. Moderate becoming good.

Epidemic:
Variable becoming death lake area 3 or 4. Love at times. Moderate.

North Decay South Decay:
Dream nectar, decreasing 5 or 6. Tranquillity. Good.

Sleep:
Marsh variable 5 to 6, becoming vapour moon. Occasional crisis. Moderate.

Death:
Cold backing sleep 5 or 6 decreasing 3 or 4. Moisture then knowledge. Moderate.

Dream:
Fertility cloud 4 or 5. Occasional heat serpent. Moderate becoming good.

Moon Hive

Nectar Love   Sex Vapour

Rainbow Hive   Dream Moon   Mist Fire

Sex Epidemic   Cold Dream   Rainbow Fire

Moisture Gate   Vapour Lake

Ingenuity Cloud   Mist Serpent

Mist Hive   Moon Heaven   Serpent Love

Cyclone Gate   Decay   Knowledge Hive

Tranquillity Freeze   Sleep Gate

Dream Fire   Sex Heat

Hive Sex   **SEARCH & REPLACE**   Freeze Bay

3 with *freeze*

Dream Area   **4** with *fire*

5 with *hive*   Vapour Gate

Crisis Fire   **6** with *sex*

Sleep Freeze   **7** with *heaven*   Love Death

Cyclone Hive   **8** with *gate*   Fertility Heat

Heaven Nectar

RANDOMISE

Dream Hive   Lake Fire

PURIFY

Sea Sleep

SAMPLE—**Emily Dickinson**

Vapour Hive   ***Within that little Hive***

Such Hints of Honey lay

As made Reality a Dream

Rainbow Heaven   ***And Dreams, Reality***

Love Decay   Hive Lake   Fire Hive

Cloud hive

Death Moon   Sleep Hive

Moisture Knowledge   Tranquillity Sleep

Fertility Cloud   Dream Serpent

Dream Nectar

REPORT: This morning, checked the hives again. All okay, except for Hive 7. What's the problem here? Perhaps the bees are merely the first to react to the new circumstances. Spent a few hours recording their behaviour. So strange. They show little interest in the carefully prepared flora, preferring instead to swarm alone to the darker reaches of the dome garden. The flowers there are stunted, ill-formed, night-blooming; the diaspora of the accelerated evolution programme. I fear the bees must starve, and yet they surely return to the hive carrying some sticky, sweet cargo. Witness: activity inside the hive is fevered, hyper; as though crisis were at hand. Watched on the monitors, amazed, as the Queen was serviced time and time again by her countless, over-fertile suitors. I felt a guilty pleasure, as though from watching a pornographic film. A dark orgy of buzz and wingbeat. In vaporous heat. Witness: the grubs are bursting the combs, grown obscene and serpentine on the brightest, thickest honey. What rainbow of wings will stir from the cocoons? Meanwhile, the workers are dancing wildly; communicating through their frenzied movements the secret locations of the nectar hoards. As they set off in search of food, I notice that the bees from Hive 2 are following them. Soon every hive will wake from sleep to perform the same ingenious dance. If I could only perfect the translation software; the patterns, the language, the cartography of the bees would be mine. Under the scope, the moon honey reveals a decayed structure; a secret flow of molecules. Witness: from the bulbous monarch of this virulent state, I have extracted a sample of royal jelly. A strange tranquillity comes over me as I examine this mutated elixir: what moist genetic knowledge must it contain? Shall I ever be brave enough to take a mouthful…

Dr Janet Plath: Moon Base IX, Sea of Clouds, 14/03/2025

Beyond the clouds, a vapour lake
This every hive believe
Along the lake, a bay of sleep
O queen this sweet receive.
A sleeping mist, ingenious
This every hive believe
Which hides from sight a moon's decay
O queen this sweet receive.
Upon the moon, a cyclone fire
This every hive believe
Within the fire, a serpent's love
O queen this sweet receive.
Inside the love, a knowledge gate
This every hive believe
Where seas of heat are tranquil found
O queen this sweet receive.
Within the heat, a moisture clings
This every hive believe
To fertilise all flowers bright
O queen this sweet receive.
A rainbow hoard of honey flow
This every hive believe
To dream the flight beyond the clouds
O queen this sweet receive.

CONTROL

OUTLET

vapour
lake

bay of
sleep

serpent
love

moon
decay

cyclone
fire

sea of
heat

moon
decay

gate of
knowing

dream
nectar

ingenuity
mist

dream
nectar

rainbow
hoard

dream
nectar

fertility
gate

dream
nectar

dream
nectar

dream
nectar

dream
nectar

tranquillity
gate

dream
nectar

moisture
gate

sex
cloud

dream
nectar

dream
nectar

crisis
hive

honey
flower

death
nectar

SAVE

'and by this key is the doorway opened'

Love's Labour's Lost

honorificabilitudinitatibus

William Shakespeare, 1595

h

o   r

            n   i

                        o

                  f   i

                        c

      a   b

                              i

            l

                                    i

                  t

      u

                              d

                                    i

                  n

      t   a

                        i

                              t

i   b

            u

                  s

HI-FI
TABU
ION
INCUBI
ID
TARO
SLIT

CDs   cassettes

loudspeakers   disco   OVERLOAD

vinyl recording amplifiers grooves DJ

radio tuner records   music faithful   veto

high fidelity low fidelity mistress unfaithful   sacred bleep out

infidelity HI-FI marriage entertainment   forbidden necrophilia curfew

affair lover precision dancing   anthropology ban paedophilia

trust   tuning loyalty   accuracy   voyeurism incest   TABU cannibalism

nightclub cuckold   frequency   illegal   coprophilia outlaw

wavelength   honour   X-rated Polynesia exclusion

amplitude   Index Librorum Prohibitorum   Satanism

shock   banned books pornography

circuit   abolition

positive negative   attraction   adults only

electricity battery particles atoms   charge   censorship bestiality

live wire spark   voodoo   witchcraft

plasma   ION electrons static   hex   demon lover wet dream

current dipole lightning   geist ghost   necromancy obeah

arc thunderstorm   enchantment   folklore monster loa

protons electrode glow amps   possession INCUBI demon

voltage ac/dc field   Midwitch Cuckoos   devil love potion

flux   exorcism love charm

discharge   nightmare sexual fantasy   sex magick

primitive   the black arts bedevilment

thanatos   dream   alien impregnation

libido   persona   spirit occultism

superego   reptilian brain

Jung   instinctive   inner darkness   ritual   the lovers

psychoanalysis Freud animus   prophecy

soul anima   ID   identity unconsciousness   caballa

psychic energies ego brain stem   justice

subconscious mind psyche   wheel of fortune

instinct identification the inner mind the devil 78 the tower cups the fool

identity card   high priestess   strength swords

brain stem   magician minor arcana 56   emperor wands

pentacles   Celtic spread Medieval Europe

fortune telling   the hanged man   reading

divination   TARO   cards empress

gap   Gypsies   major arcana 22

voyeur   temperance   chariot   hermit

opening peep   the star   high priest the last judgement

aperture chink   wound   the sun the world

nick   gash censor eyelids   death   the moon

window slice SLIT cut out rent slash tear

hole   cut   knife   scissors

keyhole operate notch rupture

breach rip   slot fissure   crevice

cleave incision sharpness

sharp split   hairline crack

groove orifice

door

The Hermit

The night is crawling with sparks. I can't sleep. Bad dreams. The heat and the sweat. Flesh prickling with itches, like Braille insects. I end up taking a three in the morning cold shower. Fifteen, twenty minutes, until the water jet weakens to a dribble. Too many people with the same idea; maybe in every room of the hotel, all the lonely people, trying to get clean.

The Star

The face in the bathroom mirror, it looks ravaged; as though something alive moves beneath the skin. I can't stop my cheeks, my right eye, the ligaments of the neck from pulsing, rapid. A demon Morse code, all over the body. I take the usual shock off the taps; electrons making their brilliant arc between metal and skin. Five minutes since the shower, it's started again.

The Tower

The window opens a two inch crack, no more. I press my mouth to the gap, breathing the night's chemical air. I'm on the tenth floor, watching all the lights flicker on and off, the crackle and buzz of the city. Lightning scissors down onto a neighbouring building, seduced by a radio antenna. The slashed air. Thunder rumbles overhead. But no rain. No fucking rain.

The Fool

The envelope. It must've been pushed under my door whilst I was in the shower. Just the room number on the front and, inside, a tarot card. It shows a young man walking blindly toward a precipice, a tied bundle of possessions over his shoulder, a small dog at his side. In the man's hand, a white flower. On the back of the card, the name of a nearby bar.

Justice
I think of ringing my wife, but the hour is late and the reasons for my leaving hardly bear explanation. All the lousy justifications come to mind; all the practised excuses. All the broken promises. And anyway, have you heard the telephones these days, with all this electricity in the air. Sure, what's the point. I gather my few things together, head for the stairs.

Temperance
A nondescript all-nighter, its name lit fitfully in spluttering neon. The Chalice. The door handle sizzles in my grip; a few more ions for the body to collect. Around a dozen people in the place, seeking to close down the dark, or start up the day. I order a soft drink, find an empty table. There's not a lot I can do, except lay the fool's card down on the table, and wait.

The Lovers
And wait; checking out the tv screen above the bar. It's logged onto a porno channel. Illicit tastes, but nobody in the place seems to be paying much attention. Luridly coloured shapes jerk and flex, as the over-excited particles interfere with the signal. I realise, finally, that one of the bodies is mine. Somebody takes the seat opposite.

The Magician
A young guy with crazy eyes, a nervous mouth, a T-shirt dark with sweat. He places a card next to mine: a robed figure holding aloft a wand; various patterned discs; a figure of eight laid flat. The guy taps at the symbol of infinity. 'I think that's meant to be a set of turntables. And this wand, that's the stylus, right? And the discs, well they're what I'm playing tonight.'

The World
We shake hands, and he gets the shock off me. 'Oh man, I thought I was suffering. Fuck. How do you live with that?' I can follow his emotions, flared in the fields of energy. And all the people in the bar, ghosted with sparks; and all the people of the world, I imagine, with their secret bodies revealed; and the Earth itself, beautiful, adorned with the aura of the ion cloud.

The Wheel of Fortune

'Look, uh, what's going on here? I mean, you got the same messages and everything, right? A bloody funny way to run a gig, don't you think? And what's with these cards? Let's see that. So, you're, uh, a comedian, that's it? I wouldn't mind, but I don't even know why I'm here? I mean, why I came here. I just had to follow the signs. Is that how it got you? Is it?'

The High Priestess

A woman sits down next to the young DJ. Her name, she tells us, is Magenta. Neat black hair, dark complexion, the distance in her eyes; all untroubled by the heat, the static. Cool blue-green waves emanate from her skin. Her card, placed on the table, shows a young woman sitting between two pillars, a crescent moon lying at her feet; in her hands, a sacred scroll.

The High Priest

The woman takes out a corresponding roll of paper. A legal contract. It binds us to secrecy, and relinquishes all responsibility on the part of the company, if anything should go wrong. We are to be paid generously, on completion of the exercise. In signing the document, the DJ notices the role I'm to take. 'Oh, so that's what you do.' And I answer, 'That's what I do.'

The Chariot

Outside, the air blisters with desire; all the atoms of the sky making brief fiery contact. A black limousine pulls up to the curb; its body is sparkled with a glow, as though a second more blissful vehicle occupied the same space. We climb inside both vehicles at the same time. Moving now, through strange, diseased streets. This isn't my city.

The Moon

Every so often a giant hoarding will beam down on us, its illuminated display teasingly coded by the surges of the power source. Magenta sits in silence, refusing to answer any enquiry. The DJ is caressing the two vinyl records she's given him, as though, by fingertip alone he could determine the mysteries hidden behind their blank white labels.

The Devil
The car pulls into the driveway of a derelict church; a building long without witness to any kind of worship, purity, ecstasy; its stained glass windows broken, gaping; the once fine stonework now cracked, and scabbed with lichen. A tall distinguished gentleman, dressed in tailored pinstripe, is waiting on the church steps. The force around his body pulses, night-black.

Strength
The studio lies below the church. A dark catacomb. Magenta works the flickering glow of an instrumentation panel; the young DJ takes his place behind a set of turntables. I am guided towards a bed in the centre of the room. I feel a strange foreboding; where are the cameras, the lights, my fellow performers? What actions will be demanded of me?

The Empress
The two records begin to play, their rhythms conjoining. A pulse of amplified blood holding a melancholic strain, tapped from some alien key. I see the music rise from the twin decks, in waves of pure energy. The melody seems to pull the air apart, forcing a wound to open. A tiny glimpse is given me, of some other world beyond this. A figure of mist floats through the slit.

The Emperor
I see now that the vinyl records are two chemicals; only under the DJ's expert fingers will they mix, forming a compound. A key. And by this key is the doorway opened. The emerging figure is a being of smoke and sorrows, taking the shape of a woman. This exquisite phantom, who drifts through the darkness towards me. Within my veins, an overpowering desire takes hold.

The Hanging Man
Desire, as the wraith flows around me. My skin is crackling with heat; all the collected ions rushing to the surface. I am charged up, an electrode of flesh; wherever this diaphanous creature touches me, arcs of positive electrons crystallise. Fountains of sparks; soft explosions in the mist. My whole body is alive in the moment, alive as never before.

Death

And there, under the gaze of all the people in that room, something accumulates within me, some ultimate rush of energy. I feel as though my organs are licked with flame, connected to the sun; a radiant pulsation that overcomes all resistance. Until, finally, all my wavelengths surge as one, and I stream forth, luminous.

Judgement

We are driven back to the city, the DJ and I, alone in the back of the limousine. We speak little to each other, both lost in contemplation. We have our money, and the two tarot cards. I cannot take my eyes off the pictured figure as it walks blissfully towards the precipice. What have I done; what edge have I stepped over? What has been lost; and what given birth to?

The Sun

We are dropped off at the all night bar. The DJ can barely look me in the eye. I take his hand in mine, gently; nothing passes between, no charge, no shock of exchange. I am drained of all voltage. Walking back to the hotel, I watch the sun come up over the city's towers. The golden orb flares briefly; and then, one by one, blessed drops of rain begin to fall.

SAVE

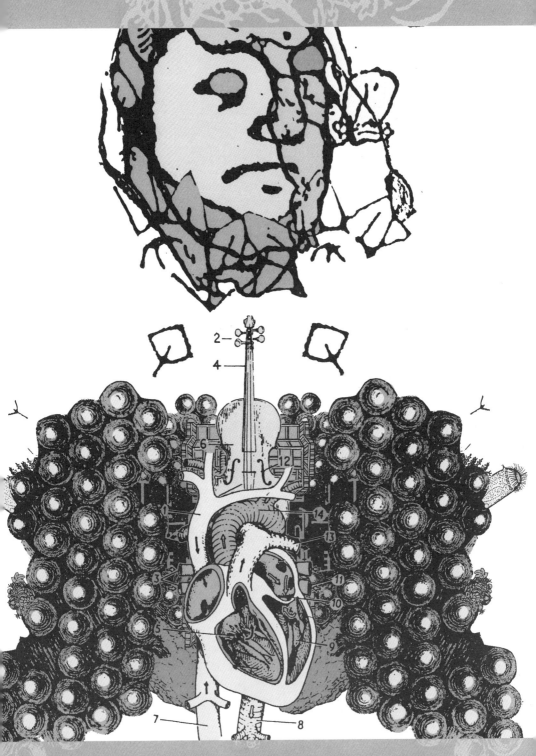

'as though the heart a violin'

Split the Lark – and you'll find the Music –
Bulb after Bulb, in Silver rolled –
Scantily dealt to the Summer Morning
Saved for your Ear when Lutes be old.

Loose the Flood – you shall find it patent –
Gush after Gush, reserved for you –
Scarlet Experiment! Sceptic Thomas!
Now, do you doubt that your Bird was true?

Emily Dickinson, 1864

Split the Lark

Find the Music

Now, do you doubt that your Bird was true?

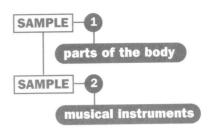

SAMPLE — 1

parts of the body

SAMPLE — 2

musical instruments

lungs   womb   stomach   tongue

ear   heart   Split the Lark   kidney   liver

bones   brain   veins   muscle

gong   castanets   double bass   violin

calliope   pianola   Find the Music   xylophone   harp

cello   snare drum   synthesiser   harp

Now, do you doubt that your Bird was true?

87

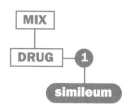

split the lark

and like a calliope, the lungs will squeeze at air
as though a pianola, the womb decodes a score
tender like a cello, all the veins are strung with care
as though a gong, the churning stomach calls for more
like the harp, a sieve of sound, the kidneys purify
as though a synthesiser, the liver's metabolic
like a double bass supporting, the muscles strength apply
within the brain like fluted notes, ideas frolic
as though the body dances on a xylophone of bone
as though the heart a violin, is tuned a notch too high
like a single castanet, the tongue will sing alone
the hearing drum a snare to catch a mating cry

find the music

now, do you doubt that your bird was true?

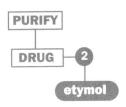

Split the Lark – **Calliope** [Gk *Kalliope* (lit. 'beautiful-voiced') the Muse of epic poetry]; **Lungs** [OE *lungen*: related to *lights*, named for their perceived lightness]; **Air** [Gk *aer*, the lower atmosphere]; **Pianola** [trademark for mechanical piano: C18 It. *pianoforte*, loud-soft]; **Womb** [OE *wamb* (ult. origin unknown)]; **Code** [L *codex* (block of wood, split into tablets: book)]; **Cello** [It. abbrev. of *violonecello*, small violone (a double-bass viol)]; **Veins** [L *vena* (ult. origin unknown)]; **Care** [OE *caru*, grief, lament (also related to Old Norse *kor*, bed of sickness)]; **Gong** [Malayan, imitative of sound made by instrument]; **Stomach** [Gk *stomakhos*, mouth of an organ (*stoma*, mouth)]; **Call** [Old Norse *kalla*, summon loudly)]; **Harp** [OE *hearpe*: related to L *corbis*, basket and Russian *korobit*, warp]; **Kidney** [ME origin uncertain: perhaps related to Old Norse *koddi*, cushion, pillow]; **Purify** [L *purus*, unstained)]; **Synthesiser** [Gk *sun*, together + *tithenai*, to place]; **Liver** [OE Gk *liparos*, fat)]; **Metabolic** [Gk *metabole*, change: from *meta*, after + *ballein*, to throw]; **Double Bass** [L *duplus*, twofold + *basis*, pedestal]; **Muscles** [L *musculus*, little mouse]; **Strength** [OE *strenge*, severe]; **Brain** [Gk *brekhmos*, forehead]; **Flute** [origin uncertain: perhaps from *lute* (Arabic *al ud*, lit. 'from wood')]; **Ideas** [Gk *idein*, to see)]; **Frolic** [Dutch *vrolijk*, happy, glad]; **Body** [Old Norse *buthkr*, box]; **Xylophone** [Gk *xulon*, wood + *phone*, voice]; **Bone** [OE *ban* (ult. origin unknown)]; **Heart** [Gk *kardia* (ult. origin unknown)]; **Violin** [uncertain origin: perhaps related to L *vitulari*, to rejoice]; **Tuned** [Gk *tonos*, tension: from *teinein*, to stretch]; **Castanets** [L *castanea*, chestnut]; **Tongue** [L *lingua*, language]; **Sing** [L *sonus*, sound]; **Drum** [Middle Dutch *tromme* (imitative origin)]; **Mating** [OE *gemetta*, dinner guest (from *mete*, meat)]; **Cry** [L *quiritare*, raise a public outcry: lit. 'call on the Quirites (Roman citizens) for help'] – Find the Music

Now, do you doubt that your bird was true?

Inside a little wooden box, lived a small mechanical mouse. He played the mouth organ, and liked to recite epic Roman poetry from a book he kept on a pedestal. Every day at noon, he sounded a gong to loudly summon his dinner guest, the lark. They dined on worm meat from tiny chestnut bowls, and grew fat and happy together. After the meal, the lark would shake her plumage, then sing in a most beautiful voice. The mouse would find the music on his instrument. The lark sang of the beginnings of words, and claimed to know where every word was born, except for womb, bones, veins, and heart. 'The heart,' she sang, 'origin unknown.'

And then one day, the lark failed to appear at the sound of the gong. The mouse tried beating on a drum, but that was no good either. He decided he must go in search of the missing guest. Over many a mile the mouse travelled, his eyes constantly searching the sky for any sign of a bird's wing, or the merest hint of a song. Eventually, he found the lark lying in the grass, moaning in pain. Her body had been split almost in two, perhaps by a cat's claw or a hunter's knife. Grief stricken, the mouse carried his friend back home, where he made a soft bed from a cushion in a basket. He tried his best to cure the lark's sickness, but nothing seemed to do any good, and the mouse's forehead was stretched with a severe tension. He raised a public outcry, calling on all the citizens to help; but none of them would. Meanwhile, the lark's body started to fall apart. The mouse tried his very best to place all the pieces back together. Eventually, however, all that was left of the lark was a tiny flickering scarlet light, deep inside, and the unstained, unflown remnants of a lament.

Now, do you doubt that your bird was true?

Well known the lark,
Well known the body's plume;
Well known, well born, well worn:
Unknown the womb.

Well known the voice,
Well known where voices start;
Well known, well cried, well tuned:
Unknown the heart.

Well known the wings,
Well known the muscle's pain;
Well known, well aired, well flown:
Unknown the veins.

Well known the song,
Well known the music's tone;
Well known, well found, well honed:
Unknown the bones.

Now, do you doubt that your bird was true?

SAVE

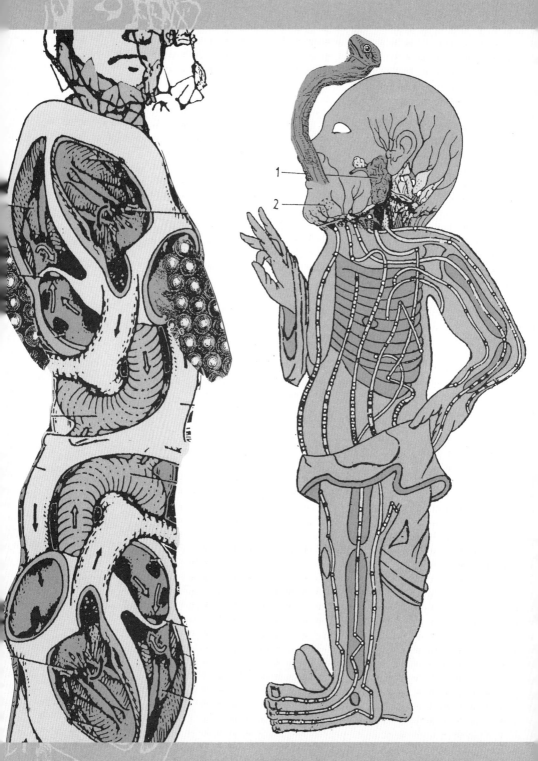

1
2

'the tongue snake thesis'

The Argument of His Book

I sing of brooks, of blossoms, birds and bowers,
Of April, May, of June and July-flowers;
I sing of May-poles, hock-carts, wassails, wakes,
Of bridegrooms, brides and of their bridal cakes;
I write of youth, of love, and have access
By these to sing of cleanly wantonness;
I sing of dews, of rains, and piece by piece
Of balm, of oil, of spice and ambergris;
I sing of times trans-shifting, and I write
How roses first came red and lilies white;
I write of groves, of twilights, and I sing
The Court of Mab, and of the Fairy King;
I write of hell; I sing (and ever shall)
Of heaven, and hope to have it after all.

Robert Herrick, 1648

I sing of   Books, of bosoms, words and blowers,
Of aerial, maze, of junk and jewel-flow;
A sign of mayday-pollen, shock-art, wails, snakes,
Of bridge-fumes, slides and their tidal quakes;
A writhing mouth of doves, and wave excess,
By thesis to sign of queenly one-tongue hex;
A sign of clues, of brains, and slice by slice
Of swarm, of spoil, of space and chamber grease;
A sign of rhyme-traps shaping, and a wraith
Of prose-thirst; flame-head and lilac night;
A flight of grooves, of twin bites, and a sigh
Of courtship mad, and of the fiery king;
A wife of spell; a sign and a fever-call
Of event and scope to save the arterial.

SAMPLE — communications alphabet

Alpha
Bravo Charlie Delta
Echo Foxtrot Golf Hotel India
Juliet Kilo Lima Mike November Oscar Papa
Quebec Romeo Sierra Tango
Uniform Victor Whiskey
X-ray Yankee
Zulu

Mayday! Mayday! Mayday!
I sing a maze of

Calling-signs; Echo Bravo, waves of junk; fever spell; Charlie's on the blower, trapped in Delta flow; swarms of prose; calling signs; spoiling the night's event – Foxtrot and Golf at the Hotel Victor; shocks in the art room; wordquake thesis; no sign of rhyme for the tongue-snake to writhe around; Romeo and Juliet, sighing, from the head to the mouth to the Mike to the antenna; calling-signs, along the bridge of ghosts; India to Quebec, sliding on Lima tides; November fumes of excess pollen; in books of blood, in books of fire; in books of grease, in wailing books of jewelled space, of lilac shape; across the mad Sierra of the brain, the court of flame; calling-signs; married to the Alphascope queen, Oscar Papa has a Uniform thirst; slice by slice, X-raying the breast of a dove; twin bites; a Kilo of Yankee Whiskey; a flight of Tango grooves; I sing of clues and ships and Zulu hex; of calling-signs and kings!

Mayday! Mayday! Mayday!

We have been but two days aboard the wreck of HMS *Juliet Bravo* and already I feel a fever spell coming over me. An unearthly atmosphere pervades the decks of this ghostly vessel, where a poster forlornly advertises a dance and a miniature golf tournament. What on earth were these able seamen doing, partaking of such arts? So many mysteries. Why did the experienced Captain Victor Romeo divert his ship from its course, all those thousands of miles towards Peru, and there to abandon it, this last November, to the tides of chance? And what of the missing crew? Did they jump ship at Lima? If some danger threatened them, why then did the captain and his father, Oscar, remain behind? If I could only connect the various clues. The captain's body, propped at his table on the bridge, his mouth on the microphone, as though he were still calling out that last distress signal. His uniform is spoiled with some kind of grease; and by his frozen hand, an empty bottle of bourbon speaks of a maddening thirst. But surely his father's scientific studies will reveal the true cause of the ship's fate. At the time of death he was examining the sliced x-rays of a dove's flightpath. The scientist's body rests on a blood-stained workbook. Most of his papers have been set on fire, but from these few pages we learn the *Bravo* was carrying a bejewelled King Cobra (quaintly named Charlie in the notes) back from India. They also made a stop at Sierra Leone, obtaining there 'certain magical items of Zulu origin', namely a kilo of pollen grains taken from a rare species of lilac flower. Also, he writes of his use of the alphascope, a device 'to reveal the secret meanings of words'. With this he claims to have uncovered something called the 'tongue-snake thesis'. In his rhymed suppositions, the dove, the pollen, and the mysterious tongue-snake are all connected. Both the scientist and the captain died of a poison, injected through twin bite-marks on the neck. The pollen swarms over everything. Of the cobra, no trace can be found, although as night closes in, I fear I can sense a certain writhing sigh behind me, sometimes a trapped and wailing echo, and then a sliding, flowing shape always just out of my vision.

PURIFY

ENHANCE

doVe

doVe

doVe

o

p

p   o

p   l   e   l

o   l   e

p   o   n

p   l

o   l   p   o

e   n

l   l   o

e   n

p   o

l   l

e   n

o

p   l   e

o   l   n

CHARLIE**O**SCAR**B**RAVO**R**OMEO**A**LPHA**L**IMA**I**NDIA**N**OVEMBER**G**OLF**U**NIFORM**S**IERRA

```
                                                          r
        c                                        a
            o            b                        s
                            a         i                        u
   c           r              l         n              g
            o            b
            b        r         i       n                s
            c        o       a      l           g             u
                        r                 i      u         s
         o        b                  a      l         n       g
         c
   o       b     r           l      i           g       u   s
      c      b            a      l       n       g         s
         o        r       a       i      n              u
   c       o     b     r     a     l     i      n     g     u        s
       c       o      b       r      l      i      n     g   s   u
         c    c    o     b     ra     l      i        n     g     u       s
         o     c     b     r     a     l     l     n     n     g  gu          s
      c     b     r     a     a     i       n     g              s
            c     o     o        b     r r   a   l   i   i   n     g           u
            c     b     r     a     l       g     u       s
               c     o     b     r     l     i   n   g     u     s
               c co  b b r r a a l i i n g u  u s
         C   O   B   R   A   L   I   N   G   U   S
```

The Argument of His Book

(eleven letter version)

I sing
In biro, in bingo, a bonus in brio,
In slogans organic, in lingo Inglano;
In cobras uncurling a glorious slurring,
Casinos, urinals, in rulings obscuring.
I sing in subsonics arousing a *largo,*
Binoculars blurring a carbonic cargo;
In scribal guano, in *logos* aligning,
In bogus albinos, all signals assigning.
I sing in Saigon, in Cairo, Bali, Sligo,
Incongruous congas, a cocoa rococo;
Illogical logic, a curious circus,
Abacus, succubus, calculus, barbarous;
Uncoiling in closing, in labouring long,
A singular boa conscribing a song.

SAVE

LAMENTING MECHANISM

'a time to pluck up that which is planted'

A time to be born, and a time to die; a time to plant,
 and a time to pluck up that which is planted;
A time to kill, and a time to heal; a time to break down,
 and a time to build up;
A time to weep, and a time to laugh; a time to mourn,
 and a time to dance;
A time to cast away stones, and a time to gather stones together;
 a time to embrace,
 and a time to refrain from embracing;
A time to get, and a time to lose; a time to keep,
 and a time to cast away;
A time to rend, and a time to sew; a time to keep silence,
 and a time to speak;
A time to love, and a time to hate; a time of war,
 and a time of peace.

Ecclesiastes, 1611 version

The blues to be born, and the blues to die; the blues to plant,
and the blues to pluck up that which is planted;
The blues to kill, and the blues to heal; the blues to break down,
and the blues to build up;
The blues to weep, and the blues to laugh; the blues to mourn,
and the blues to dance;
The blues to cast away stones, and the blues to gather stones together;
the blues to embrace,
and the blues to refrain from embracing;
The blues to get, and the blues to lose; the blues to keep,
and the blues to cast away;
The blues to rend, and the blues to sew; the blues to keep silence,
and the blues to speak;
The blues to love, and the blues to hate; the blues of war,
and the blues of peace.

The blues to be born, and the blues to die
Oh the blues to be born, and the blues to die
The blues to uproot
And the blues to water that which is dry.

The blues to kill, and the blues to cure
Oh the blues to kill, and the blues to cure
The blues to break down
And the blues to restore that which is poor.

The blues to laugh, and the blues to weep
Oh the blues to laugh, and the blues to weep
The blues to dance
And the blues to mourn the rhythm's sleep.

The blues made of stone, and the blues made of air
Oh the blues made of stone, and the blues made of air
The blues to embrace
And the blues to ignore the lover's stare.

The blues to find, and the blues to lose
Oh the blues to rend, and the blues to fuse
The blues to keep silence
And the blues to accuse, complain, abuse.

The blues in war, the blues descends
Oh the blues in love, and the blues attends
The blues of a wound
And the blues to ensure the wound is cleansed.

SAVE

DUBCHESTER KISSING MACHINE

'the city's clown is taking LSD'

A Vanishing of Grooves

oh girl / last seen dancing, to a tune unknown / & all yr friends, they lost you / deep in the grooves that night / & left the club without you / caught the cab, thinking you falling / falling in love somewhere / with some boy or some girl somewhere / to kiss & be kissed, where the night is dubbed / & even though tomorrow never brought you home, still they thought it good > until, when 4 days of silence finally / made them call the cops / oh girl / all yr friends & flatmates / relatives & colleagues / all those questions / the tears & hypertension / & maybe a smile or 2, from the ones so jealous of yr beauty / whilst down the club, & in the cloakroom hanging / yr coat was waiting, waiting / for a ticket / a claim, that never came > the place was searched, every last wave of darkness / & all surrounding areas / a dragnet stretching further, further / circles of rain, around the club, reaching out into the city / and beyond / with no body being found / & tales being told of how the girl, she was always wanting to escape / to just go floating upwards, above the weight of clouds / & perhaps she finally made it / & perhaps she never did > oh girl / yr form was caught on camera / one of 12 aimed at the floor / just a shape there, disappearing inside the crush of bass / just a moment of yr face, caught smiling / & a kiss, blown upon the data / frozen on the lens / studied / & then gone / lipstick traces / never caught again / & when the dj saw this film, his tongue was heard to say / he never played that tune, that night / he never did play that tune / there never is such a tune / there never is / never is & never is > & of all the dancers around her / only one among them, a shy & handsome boy, could remember there ever being such a girl / just a hand that was held in the crowd, & then sucked from his fingers > oh girl / last seen dancing to, a vanishing of grooves / take this hand just one more time / & kiss the rain goodbye for me / oh girl / please kiss the rain goodbye

Jeff Noon, 1999

oh girl   dancing   a tune unknown   lost   deep in the
groove   night   club   caught the   falling
love somewhere   boy   girl   kiss   kiss   the night
    dub   tomorrow never brought you
   days of silence   oh girl all yr friends &
        questions   tears & hyper   smile
  from yr   beauty   down the club   hanging
   waiting waiting   a ticket   never came   search
    wave   darkness   all surrounding   a dragnet stretching
circles   rain   into the city   beyond   no body
found   tales being told   always wanting   escape   go floating
   above the weight   clouds   & perhaps   never
oh girl   form   caught on camera   aimed the floor   shape
disappearing   crush bass   moment yr face caught   a kiss
blown   data frozen   lens   & then gone lip   traces
  the dj saw   film   tongue   never played   tune
that night   never did play   such a tune   never is never is
never is & of all the dancers   only   a shy   boy
  being such a girl just a hand   in the crowd & then sucked
   oh girl last seen dancing a vanishing groove take this
time & kiss the rain good for me oh girl please kiss the rain go d

PURIFY

ENHANCE

SAMPLE — **1**

areas of Manchester

dancing somewhere girl tune / beauty's hypergroove unknown
catch the falling lover's darkness / data frozen kissed and blown

Droylsden

escaping crush of rain god / deep in the night of bass
vanish drag and city-suck / your disappearing face

Ashton-under-Lyne

tomorrow's tales are stretching / your waiting question's kiss
the smile a dancer's body / that never is and never is

Mossley

the dj's hands in circles / tracing shape of weighted daze
down the night-lip of the dancefloor / such a tune that kissing plays

Hulme

your friends in hanging silence / with no ticket for the tongue
all surrounding wave of searching / beyond where tears belong

West Didsbury

take a dub of floating camera / in shyness of the crowd
oh dancing somewhere girl tune / this data-boy encloud

Levenshulme

danc   er girl   be   hyp   no
at   the fall   love 's dark   data   zen k   lown
            lsd
escaping rush   i g   night of bass
      drag   city suck   ing
         Ash   Lyne
ro   t   a   t   ing your waiting   ions kiss
   e   m   body a   r i   ver
          ley
e   n   circl   ing shape   h   aze
  the   lip   a tune   sing   s
        Hu me
your   hanging silen   t   tongue
a s ound   wave of sea   beyond her tears
        We   bury
     floating   ra in shyne   of the crow
   dancing   data   cloud
       vens u

SAMPLE 2
from **Crawl Town**

Was this the Escaping Game?
The beam of light was fired, and all around me
the vast engine of the Vanishing Palace stirred into noisy, clanking life.
I set my eye to ignition.

A crow shining in the rain watches as we bury the dancer's body by the river. We drag ourselves back to the vast engine of the city, along ley-lines to the palace. Now the days are empty, a cloudfall of ash hypnotises all we say and do. Even the base games of light and fire, with their ion-beams rotating, offer little escape. The city's clown is taking LSD. His sucking lips sing a Zen tune in memory of the girl; the sound waves of a kiss. Our grief is reignited, making us rush to exhume the dancer. Stirred into noise, her hanging silent tongue speaks to us. Love is the darkest data, it says, that lives beyond all tears. The crow, encircling, drops lower to pluck the tongue of Venus from our fingers. And then it floats away, vanishing into the haze.

A   shining   rain
    dance,   ourselves   the
  engine.   Now
the   cloudfall
                        games   fire
        beams   of   escape. The city's
                        lips,   a   Zen
                                    kiss
    ignited,   stir
        a   silent tongue   to   love
        the dark.   Th   e   tear
                    drops   of
  Venus,

                                vanishing.

GHOST EDIT

OUTLET

d

u

b   c   h

e

kiss

s

t

e   r

SAVE

117

COBRALINGUS: SOURCES

Organic Pleasure Engine. Completed 1 March 1999. Inlet – 'Rosalynde's Madrigal', Thomas Lodge, 1591. Sample – Jeff Noon's experiences on Sunday 28 February 1999.

Blackley, Crumpsall, Harpurhey, Saturn. Completed 1 February 1999. Inlet – 'Blackley, Crumpsall, Harpurhey', Michael Bracewell, 1999 (used with permission). Sample 1 – *A-Z of Manchester*, 1992 (note: except Wilde Street, which is imaginary). Sample 2 – *Pears Cyclopaedia*, 1997. 'Blackley, Crumpsall, Harpurhey, Saturn' was first published in *The City Life Book of Manchester Short Stories,* 1999, Penguin.

Bridal Suite Production. Completed 30 December 1998. Inlet – *Confessions of an English Opium Eater,* Thomas De Quincey, 1821. Sample 1 – *Pears Cyclopaedia*. Sample 2 – from www.cybershaman.co.uk. Sample 3 – *Frankenstein*, Mary Shelley, 1818. Sample 4 – *Pears Cyclopaedia*.

Exploding Horse Generator Unit. Completed 30 August 1998. Inlet 1 – *The Taming of the Shrew*, William Shakespeare, 1592. Sample 1 – race card, the 2.55 Maiden Stakes, Ripon, 22 August 1998. Sample 2 – *Bloomsbury Thesaurus,* 1993. Inlet 2 – *Riders of the Purple Sage*, Zane Grey, 1912 (used with permission). Sample 3 – from inlet 1.

What The Flower Holds Most Sweet. Completed 14 March 1999. Inlet 1 – *Bloomsbury Thesaurus.* Inlet 2 – The Shipping Forecast issued by the Met Office at 11.30am on Thursday 11 March 1999, broadcast on BBC Radio 4 (long wave). Sample 1 – 'Within that little Hive', Emily Dickinson, 1884.

Pornostatic Processor. Completed 10 February 1999. Inlet – *Love's Labour's Lost*, William Shakespeare, 1595. Note: *honorificabilitudinitatibus* is a late 16th Century word, a jocular form of 'honourable'.

Scarlet Experiment Song. Completed 6 March 1999. Inlet – 'Split the Lark – and you'll find the Music', Emily Dickinson, 1864. Samples 1 & 2 – *Bloomsbury Thesaurus.* Drug 2 – word origins taken from *New Shorter Oxford English Dictionary*, 1993, and *Collins English Dictionary*, 1986.

Boa Conscriptor Breeding System. Completed 8 October 1998. Inlet – *The Argument of His Book,* Robert Herrick, 1648. Sample 1 – *Bloomsbury Thesaurus.*

Lamenting Mechanism. Completed 23 February 1999. Inlet – 'Ecclesiastes', *The Old Testament*, King James Authorised Version, 1611.

Dubchester Kissing Machine. Completed 15 Jan 1999. Inlet – text original to this volume, Jeff Noon, 1999. Sample 1 – towns Jeff Noon has lived in, 1957-1999. Sample 2 – 'Crawl Town', from *Pixel Juice*, Jeff Noon, 1998, Transworld. Note: 'Dubchester Kiss' was the title of Jeff Noon's first Manchester story, published in *City Life*, 27 July 1994.

Jeff Noon would like to thank Hayley, Peter, Daniel and Michael for all their help in bringing Cobralingus to fruition.

www.cobralingus.com

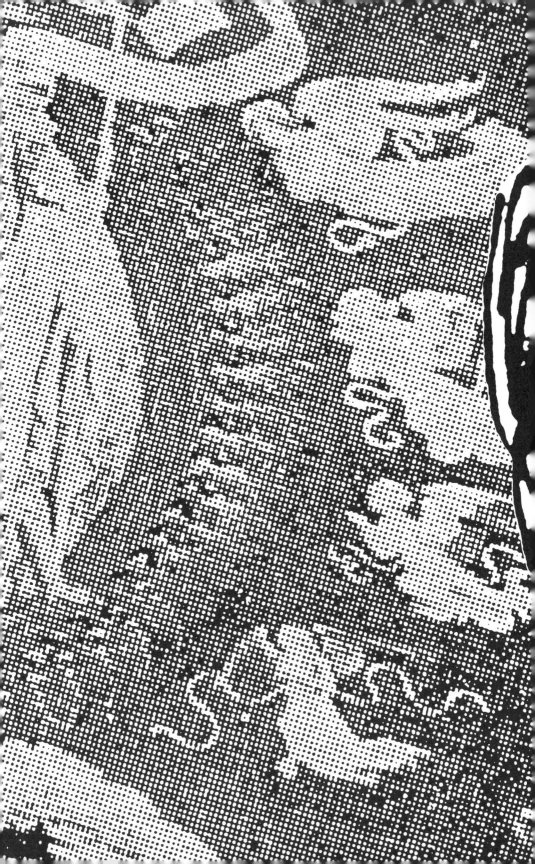

CODEX

JUNK DNA
by Tania Glyde

ISBN 1 899598 19 7 • £7.95UK • $12.95USA • $19.95AUS/CAN

In a world about to be turned upside down by the Human Genome Project, unconventional sex therapist Regina incorporates stolen pharmaceuticals into her work. Not one of her best ideas; all the women she treats develop a terrifying aversion to children. Disillusioned, she embarks on a work of scientific satire, a living exhibition of genetic poetry starting with mice and working up the evolutionary scale.

Lucy, Regina's ten year old neighbour, is a dyslexic, creative genius, born into a family on the wrong side of dysfunctional. As society starts to fall apart, Lucy quits school, orphans herself, and sets to work as Regina's assistant. Lucy becomes a very powerful little girl, and life gets more twisted by the day.

Finally, when human beings have tinkered with nature once too often, **Junk DNA** reaches an apocalyptic climax.

Provocative writer and performer, Tania Glyde is the author of *Clever Girl*. She features in the *Disco 2000* and *Vox 'N' Roll* anthologies.

'Vigorous and fluent, blackly funny and imaginative' – Literary Review

NEIGHBOURHOOD THREAT: ON TOUR WITH IGGY POP
by Alvin Gibbs

ISBN 1 899598 17 0 • £12.95UK • $19.95USA $29.95AUS/CAN • With 50 b/w photos

After receiving a call from Hanoi Rocks guitarist Andy McCoy, Alvin Gibbs of the UK Subs embarked upon a global tour with Iggy Pop. 230 nights of Iggy's unique brand of performance in just about every major town and city across six continents.

What seemed like any rock musician's dream gig became an odyssey of surreal decadence. **Neighbourhood Threat** features drugs, booze and professional Japanese groupies. Follow Iggy Pop and his band around the globe as they vomit while Johnny Thunders of the New York Dolls has wild sex on the other side of the bathroom, party hard with Guns 'n' Roses, and pretend to ignore David Bowie.

Originally published in 1995, the new Codex edition of **Neighbourhood Threat** includes previously unpublished photos, an updated Iggy Pop discography, and a new 'Outro' (an update on developments since 1995).

'Strangely compelling, frequently funny' – Vox

CHARLENE'S ANGELS
by Colin Ginks

ISBN 1 899598 15 4 • £7.95UK • $12.95USA • $19.95AUS/CAN

When queer-bashing culminates in murder somebody must take revenge...

Gus thinks everyone's out to get him – the police, the thugs at the end of the road, even Serge, the gorgeous Bosnian nymphomaniac. Will Gus come to terms with the painful side of coming out, and will he and Serge ever get it on? Or will Charlene, self-styled sex-change gangster, draft Serge into her service? **Charlene's Angels** follows Gus and his friends as they tackle the mysteries of life and death, love and loss, murder and revenge.

www.codexbooks.co.uk

CODEX

Set in Liverpool against a backdrop of saunas and nightclubs, **Charlene's Angels** is a romantic gay thriller featuring a cast of speed urchins, transsexuals and emotional refugees.

CRUCIFY ME AGAIN
by Mark Manning

ISBN 1 899598 14 6 • £8.95uk • $14.50usa $22.95aus/can • Illustrated by the author

For a decade Mark Manning was Zodiac Mindwarp, sex god, love machine from outer space and frontman of heavy metal band The Love Reaction. **Crucify Me Again** documents the spiralling depravity of his years within the moral quagmire of bad sex, worse drugs and truly horrific rock and roll.

Mark Manning has worked extensively with Bill Drummond of The KLF, co-authoring *Bad Wisdom* and the 'Bad Advice' column for *The Idler*.

'*Tales of excess and bravado imbued with a self-deprecating wit*'
– The Guardian

CHARLIEUNCLE NORFOLKTANGO
by Tony White

ISBN 1 899598 13 8 • £7.95uk • $11.95usa $19.95aus/can

CHARLIEUNCLENORFOLKTANGO is a 'stream-of-sentience' alien abduction cop novel.

CHARLIEUNCLENORFOLKTANGO is the call sign of three English cops driving around in a riot van. In between witnessing and committing various atrocities and acts of work-a-day corruption, and being experimented on by aliens, Lockie thinks aloud about old Blakie and The Sarge, cave blokes and cave birds and *Charlie's Angels.*

Tony White is the author of *Road Rage* and *Satan Satan Satan!* and editor of the *britpulp!* anthology.

'*Utterly brutal, darkly hilarious – the most remarkable novel of alien abduction I've ever read*' – Front

DIGITAL LEATHERETTE
by Steve Beard

ISBN 1 899598 12 X • £8.95uk • $14.50usa $22.95aus/can

Digital Leatherette is a surrealist narrative pulled down from invented web-sites by an imaginary intelligent agent. The ultimate London cypherpunk novel features: the Rave at the End of the World; street riots sponsored by fashion designers; a stellar-induced stock market crash; the new drug, Starflower, and barcode tattoos.

Steve Beard is the author of *Logic Bomb* and *Perfumed Head.* He has written for magazines including *i-D* and *The Face.*

'*An exuberant, neurologically-specific, neo-Blakeian riff-collage. I enjoyed it enormously*'
– William Gibson

CONFUSION INCORPORATED:
A COLLECTION OF LIES, HOAXES & HIDDEN TRUTHS
by Stewart Home

ISBN 1 899598 11 1 • £7.95usa • $11.95usa $19.95aus/can

Confusion Incorporated brings together, for the first time, the journalistic deceptions of arch wind-up merchant Stewart Home. Regardless of whether Home is being crude, rude or devious,

www.codexbooks.co.uk

CODEX

he hits his targets with deadly accuracy and side-splitting effect.

Stewart Home is the author of *Cunt, The Assault on Culture* and *Blow Job.*

'Quick, funny – the outrageous pieces leap off the page with manic energy' – Time Out

CRANKED UP REALLY HIGH
by Stewart Home

ISBN 1 899598 01 4 • £5.95UK • $9.50USA $14.95AUS/CAN

A lot of ink has been spilt on the subject of punk rock in recent years, most of it by arty-farty trendies who want to make the music intellectually respectable. **Cranked Up Really High** is different. It isn't published by a university press and it gives short shrift to the idea that the roots of punk rock can be traced back to 'avant garde' art movements.

'A complex, provocative book which deserves to be read' – Mojo

"I'D RATHER YOU LIED"
SELECTED POEMS 1980-1998
by Billy Childish

ISBN 1 899598 10 3 • £9.95UK • $17.95USA $24.95AUS/CAN • Illustrated with woodcuts and drawings by the author

"i'd rather you lied" brings together a life-time's work of one of the most remarkable and unorthodox voices of the late twentieth century. This volume sees Billy Childish take his rightful place as the poet laureate of the underdog. Includes previously unpublished poems.

A legendary figure in underground writing, painting and music, Billy Childish has published more than 30 collections of poetry and two novels,

recorded over 80 albums and exhibited his paintings worldwide.

'His poems are raw, unmediated, bruisingly shocking in their candour and utter lack of sentimentality' – Daily Telegraph

NOTEBOOKS OF A NAKED YOUTH
by Billy Childish

ISBN 1 899598 08 1 • £7.95UK • $19.95AUS Not available in the USA

Highly personal and uncompromising, **Notebooks of a Naked Youth** is narrated by one William Loveday, an acned youth possessed of piercing intelligence, acute self-loathing and great personal charm. Haunted by intense sexual desires, the ghosts of his childhood and a 7000 year old mummified Bog Man, William Loveday leads us on a naked odyssey from the 'Rust Belt' of North Kent to the sleazy sex clubs of Hamburg's Reeperbahn.

'Childish spits out vicious literary disgust in great gobbets of rancour' –The Big Issue

Coming soon:
MY FAULT

ISBN 1 899598 18 9 • £9.95UK • $15.95USA $26.95AUS/CAN

The new, illustrated edition of Billy Childish's seminal debut novel.

To order by mail, send a cheque, postal order or IMO (payable to CODEX, in UK Pounds, drawn on a British bank) to Codex, PO Box 148, Hove, BN3 3DQ, UK. Postage is free in the UK, add £1 per item for Europe, £2 for the rest of the world. Send a stamp (UK) or International Reply Coupon for the catalogue/sampler.

www.codexbooks.co.uk

steve beard
jeff noon

www.mappalujo.com

2001

if music were a drug, where would it take you?

jeff noon/needle in the groove

if music were a drug, where would it take you?

jeff noon/pixel juice

jeff noon/nymphomation

jeff noon/automated alice